WORD BIRD'S
HALLOWEEN WORDS

by Jane Belk Moncure
illustrated by Vera Gohman

Created by

THE
CHILD'S
WORLD

Library of Congress Cataloging in Publication Data

Moncure, Jane Belk.
  Word Bird's Halloween words.

  (Word house words for early birds)
  Summary: Word Bird puts words about Halloween in
his word house, introducing such words as "witches,"
"costumes," and "masks."
  1. Vocabulary—Juvenile literature. 2. Halloween—
Juvenile literature. [1. Halloween. 2. Vocabulary]
I. Gohman, Vera Kennedy, 1922-   ill. II. Title.
III. Series: Moncure, Jane Belk.   Word house words for
early birds.
PE1449.M529 1987   428.1   86-31024
  ISBN 0-89565-359-1

WORD BIRD'S
HALLOWEEN WORDS

Word Bird made a...

word house.

"I will put Halloween
words in my house,"
he said.

He put in these words—

Halloween

October 31

pumpkin patch

jack-o'-lantern

orange

black

Halloween colors

black cats

witches

brooms

scarecrow

bats

haunted house

spooks

"Boo."

owls

"Who-oo-o."

masks

monsters

costumes

parade

Halloween party

safety bug

"Trick or treat."

Halloween

Can you read these

witches

October 31

OCTOBER
1 2 3 4 5 6
8 9 10 11 12 13
15 16 17 18 19 20
22 23 24 25 26 27
29 30 31

brooms

pumpkin patch

scarecrow

jack-o'-lantern

bats

Halloween colors

haunted house

black cats

Halloween words with

Word Bird

?

spooks

costumes

"Boo."

parade

owls

"Who-oo-o."

Halloween party

masks

safety bug

monsters

"Trick or treat."

31

You can make a Halloween
word house. You can put
Word Bird's words in your
house and read them too.

Can you think of other Halloween
words to put in your word house?